Up Your Asteroid!

A Science Fiction Farce

UP
YOUR
ASTEROID!

A SCIENCE FICTION FARCE

C. EVERETT COOPER

R. REGINALD

THE Borgo Press

SAN BERNARDINO, CALIFORNIA

MCMLXXVII

Frontispiece by Roger Broadfoot.

Library of Congress Cataloging in Publication Data

Cooper, C. Everett
    Up your asteroid! A science fiction farce.

    I. Title.
PZ4.B95713Up   [PS3552.U7147]   813'.5'4   77-866
ISBN 0-89370-206-4

R. Reginald, The Borgo Press is a wholly-owned subsidiary of
Lynwyck Realty and Investment Company, Inc., P.O. Box 2845,
San Bernardino, CA 92406.

First Edition-----April, 1977

For

Steve and Gina,

who will appreciate it.

And also for:

Clark Smith, Ginger Melrose, Peter & Lori Briscoe, Brother Mark, Mary Swisher at age 100, Richard Marchand, S.J., Holly Sullivan, the Great Hound Nebuchadnezzar, R. Reginald, Roxana Daetwiler, Mac Hulke, Doris Illes & Rex, Steve Romage, Denny Maloney, Doug Menville, Capucine and the ghost of Neferkitty, Terry Callan, Michael Grainey, my *mother-in-law*, George & Dany Slusser, the Count of Monte Cristo, Anne Provost, Barry R. Levin, Franz Schneider, Scott Coble, S.J., Barry Andrews, David Compton, Roland Green, Gordon & Kay Johnson, Fax Fay Faz, Ganpat, Liz Fishman, Frances Ekaitis, Margaret Summers, Tom Crawford, S.J., Fran Polek, Joe Chouinard, Linda Miller, Denise Gipson, Alice Wilson, Piers Jacob, Willie Morris, Richard Mathews, Susan the Sheep, Frank Campbell, Rae O'Dell, Saki, Eric Eddison, Peter Spader, Brother Scott, Mom & Dad, Bruce Golden, Sobhuza II, Dick Haskell & Friend, Mike & Nancy Downing, J. Michael Reaves, Count Dracula, Al & Daryl Saunders, the Comte d'Alver, A. M. H. J. Stokvis, R. Lionel Fanthorpe, Dinizulu, Leslie Barringer, Leslie Kay Swigart, H. Rider Haggard, Allan Quatermain, Ben Ramsey, She, Linda Snyder, Tarzan, Cliff Wurfel, Greg Robbins, St. Coleslaw of Lwow, Roger Broadfoot and Megan, and all the boys and girls down at CSCSB.

But most of all for

My Wife.

Once upon a time to come, a little girl lived down the lane from Fields, Missouri, not far from the peanut factory. Her name was Miss Vajinah Wolfe. Miss Vajinah's mother had died of constipation and sunstroke years before, while working out in the peanut fields, and Miss Vajinah's father was the famous turkey baron, Col. Lupus Wolfe, Esq., B.V.D., who boasted of having his Missouri Fried Turkey franchises in every hovel and chapel in the universe. Miss Vajinah was as ugly as southern sin, like an aardvark with buck teeth and ingrown toenails, and everyone knows how ugly they are. And being the only child of an only child of an only child twenty-five times removed, she was the last of her line, and her daddy very much wanted her married off.

"Sweetie," he would beg. "I jes' gotta have me a grandson to carry on th' line. Cain't ya jes' try a little bit for your poppa's sake?" And Miss Vajinah would simper up her lips, put her frail arms around Big Daddy's husky shoulders, nuzzle his spare tire, pull on his snowy-white beard, and whisper softly into his ear: "But Daddy, I jes' don't know *how*!" And that would be that. There came a day when the latest in a long line of suitors, disappointed and damned, was crabbing his way out the side door, when Col. Wolfe grabbed him by the shoulders, and hustled him into his library, which was filled with row upon row of books on turkey farming and peanut growing. "Now son," he groused, "Now son, you-all comes from good old Suthrun stock, and you ain't got much more than those slick patent shoes you-all's wearin', and I got this-here check for a million peanut-shells, if'n you marries my one true daughter. Now what you-all got to say to that, huh?" The poor man hummed and pawed, and finally blurted out: "Well, you see, sir, she's got, uh, nothin' up front." The old frigger turned a brilliant orange: "Jackson," he yelled. "Suh." "Take this-here piece of white trash, and feed him to the dogs." "Yassuh." And another fair-haired son of the South found his way into doggie litter. This was the 36th time the hounds had had southern fried dessert, and Col. Wolfe was beginning to suspect something was wrong somewhere. So he called in a dermatologist, and then an orthodontist, and a chiropractor, and a veterinarian, and finally a hemoflagellate, but nobody seemed to know what to do. So finally his despair overpowered his stern self-control, and he told Jackson to fetch Mammy Jumbo, the witch doctor.

There was a shakin' of the ground, and the smell of black-eyed peas acomin' through the air, and a roarin' like 42 tornadoes all meetin' together in a convention somewheres, and then Mammy Jumbo appeared. "Who-all's disturbin' the rest of Mammy Jumbo?" shrieked the wind. Lupus Wolfe fell to his knees. "I-i-i-it's j-j-jes' m-me, the poor turkey farmer down th' road," came his reply, "And Mammy, I surely needs your help." "Don't you go on mimickin' that Black talk to me, you honkey Uncle Tom. I knows jus' what you wants, and you wants it real bad too; so you better be pretty damn nice wit' me, or that ugly daughter of yourn ain't never gonna do nothin' with nobody. Now jus' whatya gonna give me in return, peanut face?" The old plantation farmer jumped to his feet: "Jackson," he roared, "Get me my stash of Kruegerrands." "But suh, dey weys a ton." "You heard me, Jackson." "Yassuh," he sighed, and back he staggered, an hour later, bent over double with the load on his back. "Cotton was better," he muttered, as he spilled them all over the floor.

Big Daddy Wolfe picked up one of the yaller coins, and waved it in the Mammy's face, with a look in his eyes that shouted out in 12-point English Bold, "Pretty Please." "Take them," he cried, "Oh take them all, but get my daughtah a new set o'knockers, and then get her married off to the one of her choice." Mammy Jumbo shook her salt-and-pepper curls, and chuckled as she scooped up the loot: "You asked for it, honey. And now I does it."

The money vanished up her apron; then she drew from between her pendulous breasts a cream-colored globe, and wiped off the scum with her sleeve, revealing a clear, plain piece of glass. Waving her greasy fingers over the ball, she chanted: "Mammy Jumbo, thick and dumbo, chicken soup, produce da gumbo!"

Suddenly the room went dark, and beneath the two white spots that marked the Mammy's ivory eyes, the glass began to glow with a purplish hue, like the color of a man being garrotted. A violet odor filled the room, and there was a sharp crack, like the snap of a baseball bat. Suddenly the lights came on, and standing where the witch had been was a large, purple, six-foot high toad, wearing a strange sort of harness over his warty body. "Oh my," it lithped, "Oh my goodneth, what have we here. Thenthienth Beingth, could you tell me the way to Eath Bombay?"

Lupus Wolfe nearly died then and there, and would have too, but for the fact that he had an income tax rebate coming. "Jackson," he snorted, "Jackson, what the friggin' hell is dat!" The old lackey shuffled over, mutterin' to hisself: "Well, suh, it looks to me like a native of the Beta Beta Chapter of the Alpha Beta Digamma system." And sho'nuff, it was. Meanwhile, the toad was doing something disgusting on the ballroom floor. "She-it," cursed the Colonel, "Haven't you aliens ever learned how to use the outhouse. Ke-rist. Jackson, the mop." "Yassuh," muttered the slave, "What I gots to do to earn mah pension..."

Then Wolfe turned to the thing sitting in the middle of the floor: "You-all listen to me, you four-legged fruit; I'm the boss of this here spread, and you jes' hand over that passport to me, or I'll blow you-all full of peanut shells. Savvy?" The creature was obviously disturbed, and making all sorts of obscene and disgusting noises from various orifices. "Oh lookit, lookit, you're making my deodorant run all over the plathe, you big meanie, you. What ith thith univerthe coming to!" The toad drew a plaque out of its mouth, and tongued it over to the portly landowner. "Oh my, you are a big one, aren't you now. Oh my yeth, you barbarianth are thoooo handthome." The Colonel's stomach flipflopped: "You-all keep away from me, you hear? Now, you jes' listen good: I got this-here passport, and you ain't goin' nowheres, unless'n I says so. And you-all is goin' to do me a real favor, and make me grateful enough to give it back to you, unless I reneges. My byutiful daughter, Miss Vajinah, my only begotten hun, needs a couple of big ones to get a hubby, and by my twin silver bullets, you-all's gonna find 'em for her. Now get your ass movin', you hear?" "Yaththuh," saluted the strange being, and he drew out of his anal passage an aluminum device fitted with tin antennae, which bore the strange label: *Captain Super's Astro-Finder.*

Twiddling a few ninnies produced no results, so he freebled his bean, and sure enough, there was a warbling of the vapours, and a mixing of the ethers, and suddenly a voice came surging through:

> *"I am the Captain of the Intercourse,*
> *I have a merry crew.*
> *They're very very weird,*
> *And very very queer,*
> *And they don't know what to do.*
> *But whenever they're in doubt,*
> *They only have to shout,*
> *For the leader of the few.*
> *And wherever I may be,*
> *In whate'er capacity,*
> *I bid them all adieu.*

So give three cheers without remourse,
For the hearty Captain of the Intercourse.
Yes, give three cheers without recourse,
For the Captain of the Intercourse!"

"Somewheres I've heard that one before," the Colonel grumbled. "Yath," the creature chirped, "They jutht don't theem to have much variety on the galactic airwavth anymore." Then, bringing the signaller close to his warty throat, he thrieked: "Oh help. Oh help. Oh rapine and flower-dethroyerth. Oh thave me from a mate worthe than death! Thith ith the being Nethtor, calling from the Planet Earth." Turning to the plantation master, he noted, "Gentlebeing, pleathe be ready to leave with your daughter in thikthteen micromegonth." When Wolfe returned with daughter and servant in toe, the alien was trembling with anticipation: "They come. Oopth: we go." There was a tingling in their blood, like the after-effects of three orgasms in a row, and the mansion was suddenly empty.

Junius T. Shark, Commanding Officer, U.S.S. Intercourse, was sitting quietly in his command chair, diddling Yeoperson Randy, when the frantic call came up from Receiving. "Arghh," cracked the communicator, instantly waking half the Bridge crew. "Captain," Oyoohoo sibyled, "We have a message from Receiving." "So I heard," he sighed, and dumped the unsuspecting girl onto the cold hard deck, where she gazed up at him with lambeth eyes. "Oh Captain, my Captain, the race is nearly won." "Oh shit," quoth the captain, and immediately got down to Syria's business: "Interpretations, anyone?" Pox raised his languid brows from where he sat, perched high on the science consol: "In prognostication, Captain, the individual being considered is not the average alien from whom statistics have been compiled; however, innocent grass may conceal smoke, and to destroy the false profit,

one must first unmask it before the eyes of the true believers.''
The Vulgarian once again lapsed into that strange, silent, emotion-
less state that always accompanied his many personal failings;
although he never seemed to draw much strength from the inhuman philosophy that characterized his native world, he was still
fond of quoting the old aphorism, *Great pain follow great happi-
ness follow great pain.* ''You're not helping,'' Shark shrieked,
and he jabbed his stubby thumb down on the yeoperson's button:
''Shoddy, what the hell's going on down there!''

But at that crucial moment, the escalator doors flew open, and
the great bulbous body of the alien Nethtor hopped through, followed by Lupus Q. Wolfe, his six-guns erect in his fleshy hands;
holding up his rear was Miss Vajinah, and trailing along behind,
buried under a tomb of luggage, was the angel Jackson. It was
Wolfe who took the lead, waltzing over to the command chair with
a-one and a-two, scu-bee-doo-bee-doo: ''Hey you-all, what's
your rank, boy?'' Momentarily unplussed, Shark replied strait-
forwardly: ''I am the Captain of the Intercourse, I have a mer....''
''Well, now seein' as how I'm a Colonel in the Missouri Brigades,
I outrank you, and I am orderin' you, suh, to step down from that-
there chair, and sit in this-here chair, so's I can sit in that-there
chair, and you can sit in this-here chair, etcetera. You got that,
boy?'' Shark was unable to refute the utter logic of it all in his
mind, so he got.

Lupus Wolfe settled his huge bod onto center stage, and then ro-
tated in a slow circle: ''Now, you boys is workin' for me, you
hear? We-all do things a li'l diffrent in the South. First thing
we're gonna do is change the name of this-here boat. We gonna
call it the *Dingdong Belle,* aftra mah dear dead mothah. Second
thing we gonna do is move things round a li'l. You there, boy,
what's your name?'' ''Ensign Kulli, sir.'' ''Well, Kulli, I'm gon-

na make you a real big man, see: you-all's gonna get to do mah laundry. Now you there, you-all's black. What are you doin' up here." Oyoohoo crawled out of the depths of perdition: "Why, I'm Communications." "Hee hee, well now, you-all can communicate real personal with me, you hear?" Then, looking over to where Pox marked time in little sections carved into his aperture, he noted: "Boy, you-all is the strangest thing I ever seen, outside of this-here thing doin' his mess on the floor. Lordie, that is the messiest toad I ever did see. Now, you jes' get a mop, and clean it all up, like a good alien.

"Now you folks list'n to what I gotta say. We-all's goin' to reorganize, see, accordin' to the good old American principles called Management by Objections. That is, everytime I orders someone to do somethin', you gotta write down jes' what you-all thinks of it, an' then I shows you-all where you're wrong. And then you gotta say whatchya gonna do with your career, and why, so's I knows what's goin' on in all your heads, and I can chop 'em off if'n I needs to. And every so often, I'm gonna bring each and every one of you into my office, and discuss it all with you interminably, so you-all knows I'm a good manager. Meanwhile, I'm gonna fill this galaxy full of fried turkey huts." Miss Vajinah finally understood that something was up: "Daddy, what's a galaxy?" she piqued portentiously. Wolfe ignored her, as he had learned to do over the years; it wasn't that he disliked his only child, but he realized that her mental capabilities were something less than zero. Instead, he turned his manly attentions to the toad: "Wart-face, where the hell you takin' us?"

The alien had by this time found a common interest with his comrade-in-arms, Astrogator Pox, who was engaging him in a lengthy conversation about the young boys of Pi R II. Startled from his ecstatic reveries, the amphibian noted: "Oh tender keep-er of the keyth, the only thingth that can thave your daughter--prethiouth girl--are the *Guardianth of Titteroth*, a planet near the Betelgeuthe offramp on the other thide of the Galaxy." "Daddy, what's a galaxy?" Wolfe fingered his thing contemplatively: "OK, so you-all gonna take us there. Now getch yournselves movin'." And he fired a couple of shots into one of the technicians fixing the light boards. Shark finally found the courage to speak up: "Sir, I beg to point out to you that this is a vessel of the United System of Stakhanovists, and that we have a three- or five-year mission to perform, depending on how you count them. We just can't go off on some wild turkey hunt for a mere individual or two; it's gotta be something important, like the lives of thousands or millions, before we can even press the starting button. Otherwise none of us will get our gold stars, or our genuine cows-foot good-luck charms this year. Besides which, what will momma say?"

At which point the overloaded emotion circuits in the Captain's feeble mind broke down entirely, and Miss Vajinah commented, "Daddy, what's a galaxy?" "She-it, won't somebody tell her, and shut her up," yelled the Colonel. It was Pox who perked his twin antennae over the horizon, and murmured: "Galaxies like grains of sand. Strangers in their own lands. Three dollars and twelve quarters. The galaxy is like a grapefruit tree, fragrant in the summer wind, filled with green and browning fruit, each one a little star budding forth or half-mildewed. Yea, the stars are ripe forever, and we are fed with silent food." "What's with that boy?" Wolfe asked the Captain. Shark grinned knowingly, his eyes full of 10^4 thoughts: "He's a bit off."

Truer words were never spoken, for at that moment, the communicator suddenly came to life, and bit the outstretched hand of Mistress Oyoohoo. "Captain," she cried, trembling with pleasure and pain, "we have a signal coming in on the view-screen." Yeoperson Randy tried to grab the officer by his half-masted trousers, but he managed to kick her grasping fingers away with a few whispered endearments: "Later, love, later. I have battles to fight, promises to keep, and miles to go before we sleep together." Her eyes revolved like ping-pong balls: "Oh Jun, you're so mythopoeic," she breathed. "So I am," he acknowledged modestly, and pushed Wolfe backwards over the command chair: "You will excuse me, Colonel, but you're not trained to handle a situation like this. As soon as the danger is past, I'll let you have the conn again."

Gazing intently around the command room, Shark noticed the intent gazes of his crew gazing back intently into his intent eyes. "What's the situation, Fuckoff?" he inquired. "Comrade Captain, we have been ordered by the Kringles to surrender unconditionally, or be shot out of the wery sky we are trawersing. The fascist bourgeois insect has reared its ugly head again in intergalactic space. We must wipe this parasitic menace...." But his words were fortunately lost to posterity, as the *Dingdong Belle* was struck amidships by a three thousand ton iron ball. "Damage reports," screamed Pox. "Here, here, here," answered the crew, hoping to reach sickbay, and the waiting arms of Nurse Couple. "What was it, Pox?" asked the Captain, struggling to preserve his cool. The serene countenance of the Vulgarian peered up from his gaily decorated corner: "Explanation is a palliative, not a cure, Captain. Truth like olive oil will in time rise to the surface. By the way, you have blotchies under your armpits." "Ring around the collar," they all chimed in. In the background, Jackson was strumming his banjo, and softly singing:

Starship Captain sing dis song, do-dah, do-dah
Kringle cruiser five-mile long, oh do-dah-day

Gonna run all night,
Gonna run all day,
Bet mah money on da Kringle ship,
Dey gib dere men mor pay.

"Christ," said Shark, "things haven't been this bad since the Oregonians started levying income tax. Give me lights and action, Oyoohoo." There promptly appeared on the viewscreen that long-running feature, *The Alien Ways,* with the hoots and applause of the crew, which rapidly changed to boos as the heavy appeared. "I am Kurnel, Kaptain of the Kringle Kruiser *Kwork,* and member of the Krude Klucks Klan of the Kringle Konfederation. I have brought to my attention this one noteworthy fact, that you are contemplating an infringement of our monopolyright on fast food franchises throughout the Galaxy, a term which I will explain to no man, and despite the fact that Kroid recommends instant punishment and detergent reaction to threats of this nature (see sections *PS648.S3* and *PN6071.F25*), I/we are inclined to be generous to first offenders, and to destroy them only lightly, giving you three unusually gentle alternatives: complete surrender, target practice, or thirty virgins prime and tender, with plenty of filet. You needn't respond till tea-time." And he vanished into the haze. "Smokey's out," Wolfe noted, hiding behind the lavatory. "So are the thirty virgins," noted Shark, "At least in this galaxy." "There's that word again," sighed the ugly one with the slim hips and flat chest. Pox, however, was the practical sort, and he began checking up on the obvious: "Sir," he demoted, "This may be important. Tea-time begins in just two minutes, 29 seconds."

In a lesser man, fear might have overcome his iron control, but Captain Shark was built with different sticks and stones, so he just shit in his pants. "What shall I do?" he asked the winds. Pox, as always, was ready with a remedy: "Try some Helter-Skelter, sir; it's good for organic distress, particularly when you only have one minute, 42 seconds remaining before everyone becomes so much cosmic dust. Verily, patience sometimes leads to knowledge, but in hesitancy, the easier the diagnosis, the worse the prognosis." "Organic distress, huh?" quoth the Captain: "Pox, you're a genius! Oyoohoo, get me the Oregonians on line three."

"One minute, 22 seconds, sir." The blackwoman stirred out of her natural liturgy: "What was that, sir?" "One minute, 9 seconds." "Shut up, Pox," Shark raved, "Shut up, alla you. Just leave me alone. I never really wanted to be Captain, anyway. Oh bales of peas! Get me the fuckin' Oregonians on line three, Oyoohoo, or I'll have your paycheck cashiered out." The blackess plugged her lines into the console, and reported: "Sir, they need the area code." "Oh, shit." "I can smell it, sir, but they refuse to make exceptions." "I think it's 503--try 503, OK?" "Yes sir." "Thirty-nine seconds, Captain." "Captain," sparked Oyoohoo, getting a charge out of a shortcircuit in the panel, "Captain, I think it's coming, oh Captain, I know it's coming, oh please Captain, help me, oh oh oh, *I MADE IT!!!*"

An old man in flannel pjs sat up in bed. "Fee fei fo fum, I'm sure as hell getting tired of phone calls at three o'clock in the morning. Jeezus, what is it now? Who the hell are you freaks in the funny suits, and what do you want at this miserable hour, anyway? Christ, a superhuman being can hardly get any sleep anymore. And you all want advice for free, too. Not a damn one of you ever pays. The phone bills alone...." "Ten seconds, sir." Shark stumbled in: "Sorry to interrupt, your excellency, but we've got a problem here, and there's a bit of a time difficulty attached; please get these Kringles off our tails." "Oh screw the

Kringles," the ancient wonder remarked, and pulled the sheets back over his head. The grim visage of the Kringle Kommander appeared once again on the screen: "I'll get you for this, Shark, if it's the least thing I ever do." Two more thingamajigs struck the *Dingdong Belle*'s overloaded screens, and then a great, brown, amorphous lump was expelled from the rear of the fleeing enemy ship, wholly engulfing the good guys in sticky sludge. "What happened?" Shark inquired introspectively. Dr. Hoyle burst onto the bridge: "It was lust," he cried, "lust, lust, lust. They were overwhelmed by the orgy of it all, ha ha. Lust is the power of the universe. Lust is what made each and every one of us the sinners we are today. I'm lust, you're lust, even that disgusting amphibian, fruity as it is, is lust."

But the minister's reminiscences (later published in six volumes by Rutters University Press) were interrupted by a measure of sanity as the vessel settled into orbit around Circus III, with its three interlocking golden rings glowing brightly in the setting horizon of the tristar, throwing their incandescent messages through the unfathomable reaches of space. Pox cried at the sight, remarking semintelligibly, "When eating a roach, a sensitivity reaction may be due to a past event as well as a present disturbance." It was a poignant moment for all. Wolfe was on the verge of taking control of himself when Oyoohoo reported a distress signal from the planet's surfaces. Before anything happened, he managed to ask: "Do you-all get many of these calls?"

"Only about once a week," Shark responded, "Although certain ones do seem to turn up over and over again. Status report, Oyoohoo." "Captain, it's the Kringles again. They're setting up Krusti Fried Chicken huts all over the planet, and using them to subvert the catholic missionaries sent by Pope Joan III to enlighten the population. There've been a number of mass eatings in which churchmen have been fricaseed into catholic stew, and later eaten in holy orgies of gluttenous maximus.'' There was a sudden intake of breath amongst the Bridge crew. ''Leap for the Lord,'' shouted Lt. Zwingli, and there was a mad rush for the outhouse, still jealously guarded by Colonel Wolfe. Shark ordered an immediate survey party, consisting, as usual, of himself, Pox, and Dr. Hoyle, the resident theologian and snake charmer. ''You're in charge,'' the Captain shouted as he fled down the escalators, ''And don't blow it, either.''

The intrepid explorers materialized fifteen feet up in a Circus tree, a not uncommon experience when the masterful engineer was manipulating the controls. ''Gee, Captain,'' quoth the quack, ''Do you remember the time when....'' ''Indeed I do, Hoyle,'' he replied graciously. ''Now, which way do we go?'' Pox somberly regarded the setting suns: ''If I may make a suggestion, sir, I think it might be best if we descended to ground level before proceeding further on a straight line. A long road is sometimes the shortest path to the end of a journey; however, severe sensory dislocation is symptomatic of amnemonic transmigration, and should be reduced to zero as soon as possible.'' ''Obviously,'' Shark replied. ''Pox vobiscum.'' ''Et cum spirits toot-toot oh,'' they all chanted. ''Sir,'' Pox noted, ''I have a confession to make.'' ''Later, Pox, later; we're being menaced again.''

As indeed they were, if pitchforks and torches were any indication; the natives were restless tonight. A particularly vicious-looking barbarian (the one with fangs, hairy hands, and a moth-eaten ape suit), stepped forward: ''I arrest you in the name of the Popular Provisional Peoples' Party Progressive Prevolutionary Prepublic of Pringlington, on whose ground you are so daintily trespassing, having been charged with the sins of selflessness, charity, refusing to support the clergy, adherence to doctrine, and a general disregard of immoral principles; in addition, I find about you a certain repugnant odor, as one might associate with the unwashed masses." Which was not wholly untrue, since the hearty men and women of the 29th century had dispensed with baths as being unhealthy and wasteful of water. "By the way, I fancy those thingies you've got there on your saddle belts; purely as a matter of scientific curiosity, could you explain to me how they work? Pox, ever the eternal boy, was eager to show his superiority over native intelligence, so he quickly pulled out a quaser and communicator, and turned them on. In the process, only three and a half natives were incinerated, a small loss under the circumstances. "Fascinating," the barbarian remarked; "It must work something like this." Levelling the quaser at a heavily-bound girl who was being dragged through the brush as an anchor, he fried her where she lay. "Not bad," he noted, "but definitely inferior to the Kringle Mark IV." "You monster," shouted Doc Hoyle, straining wildly against the civilized part of his nature, "Just let me loose, and I'll tear you into little shingles with my bare knuckles." The alien motioned with his elbow, and the ropes fell at the minister's feet. "Uh, well," he sublimed, "I'm sorta out of practice, if you know what I mean. Maybe next week, or the week thereafter?"

The barbarian squatted down on his thick green tail. "Do not judge us, oh Shirik, until you hear this, our side, of the story. I am Salgoud Ellivnem, leader of the revolutionary movement. Many moons ago, as you reckon time, an evil man, Edie Amino Acids, overthrew the traditional tripartite government of Circus, executing all the political leaders he could find, and eating the rest. After changing the name of the republic to Duglanda, he instituted a religious dictatorship, subverting the masses in a panacea of opiate services. At first, the new regime was welcomed with smuggled arms, for the previous rulers were harsh and humorless, and we Circusians like a good joke with the rest of them. Edie Amino Acids understood this, and made the government a joke. But then his true nature began to emerge, and the Grand Monk, as he now called himself, began placing catholics in all the key governmental positions, mixing in Angricans, Prest Syberians, and even Sodomists and Gommorites. The people were shocked by this open worship of the gods, and were forced to participate in this perversion of dictatorship by voting for the candidates of their choice, and sometimes even running for office themselves. Our previously unrestrained capitalistic society was severly restricted, with businesses forced to spend millions of donutos installing safety devices for the workers; pension plans and decent wages were made mandatory, and decent housing was constructed for the hordes of uneducated peons joyously working for the good of the state.

"It was a crisis of massive hoi pollution. Rich men became paupers overnight; the price of food plummeted. To dampen the public unrest, Acids called in the Kringles, who set up hut after hut of cheap chicken friers, apparently thinking that all this free food, and the unsightly entertainment occasioned by wholesale executions of non-catholics, would mollify the people. Well, sir, we were not fooled by these deceptions. A few followers of the Holy Toad--glorious be his name--escaped to the countryside, forming miniscule resistance groups seeking to restore our traditional excesses of government. Will you join us in this eternal struggle to restore autocracy?" The alien simultaneously shifted his quaser to cover the Captain's midriff bulge, and held out a battered tin cup. "I think we can be persuaded," noted the Captain laconically, and so the spacemen from the *Dingdong Belle* became diehard revolutionaries, fighting for the cause of rampant injustice.

They planned their strategy while getting stoned out of their minds in a little native hut. "Now that we have these weapons," Salgoud Ellivem commented, "we should be able to clean up the Capitol sometime this afternoon, and grab the rest by tomorrow morning." "Yo," shouted his followers in unison, "Ho. Yo ho. YO ho ho." Shark was puzzled by one detail, however: "Your maps seem to indicate that the capitol city is quite some distance away; how are we going to get there by this afternoon, when it's already dusk?" "You're right, Captain," jumped the alien, and banged the poor officer over the head with his gorgeously green tail. "So we'll have din-din instead." After the smoke had settled to the ground, Shark remarked: "It's very good, but a little bland for my taste. What is it?" Salgoud Ellivnem chortled in his broth: "Boiled Christian, with vegetables and mushrooms. Takes care of the disposal problem, you know."

Pox was impressed: "Captain, they may have something here. A hasty conclusion, like a hole in water, is easy to make, but hard to maintain." His voice lowered to a whisper: "Still, I wonder if we are not violating the Prime Direction." As every good space-man knows, Spacefleet Command required that no interference be made with native cultures unless there was the possibility of a profit somewhere. "Of course," Shark noted, "if we re-place the Kringle Kitchens with Wolfe's Missouri Fried Tur-key franchises...." A glowing light illuminated the scene, as a bomb was dropped on the adjoining camp. Within an hour's time, the rebels had boarded the Pringlington Municipal Special, and were speeding towards their rendezvous with destiny. Their tar-get was the chief headquarters of the chicken chain, Kringle Klutch #1. Pox commented surreptitiously: "Sir, I've been watch-ing the motored vehicles used in this ecosystem, and it occurs to me that if I could have access to the engine compartments, I might be able to construct a communications transmitter out of the electric wave receiving sets each presumably contains, provided that a real benefit is to be derived from doing so." "Pox, you're a genius," the Captain exclaimed. "There is a 99.52% probability of that being so," he agreed, and he began watching for his opportunity.

The chicken hut was shaped like a large square box, with four sides and a roof, painted white, with red and blue markings, and topped with the huge, naked image of a headless chicken with its shaved legs spread wide. "By Jiminy," Hoyle said, "I never realized how disgusting these fiends really were. To subject poor innocent children to such obscene depictions of sex and cruelty, when they should have been reserved for consenting adults; it's horrible, horrible."

The rebel forces were disguised as garbagemen, so they passed the Klutch without being seen. Just before the attack began, Shark noticed a little sign tucked above the door: *over 5.4 x 10 to the 19th power served*. He wondered how many had died as a result.

His reveries were disrupted by the impressive sound of fizzles doing their thing, and as the bodies of scattered patrons began littering the streets, the surprised Kringles began returning their fire. "I've been hit," shouted Ellivnem. He stared down at his bloody arm in disbelief: "My Toad, they're using splintered chicken bones in their shells." And he promptly began returning tit for tat, throwing disgarded pieces of rotten chicken back into the faces of the public defenders. The battle soon degenerated into a Mexican standoff, with bodies of dead and decaying Mexicans being propped up in the Klutch's windowsills to ward off the evil eye. "We've gotta get some help," Shark whispered into Pox's attentive ears, and the alien wandered off through the chunks of shattered Circusians, pausing now and then to pocket jewelry and watches. Eventually, he worked his way over to a late-model vehicle, and jimmied open the door.

Meanwhile, back at the brunch, the struggle was growing more desperate, as defenders and attackers alike ran low on ammunition. Just as Shark was about to surrender, the golden glitter of reinforcements began to solidify in the crossfire zone. There, squatting on a platform of his own, was the giant bulk of Nethtor, the usual rivulets of crud seeping out from under his huge frame. "Greetingth, gentlebeingth, wherever you are," he hissed, and the firing ceased. There were cries of "The Holy Toad," and "The Amphibian comes to claim his own," as the defenders threw down their chicken bones, and rushed out to be systematically exterminated by their victors.

But Shark suspected a trap, and pressed forward towards the Klutch. silhouetted against the cream-colored sky was the Kringle Kommander, Kurnel, whom he had vanquished scarcely three days before. "Curse you, Shark," the alien shouted, as he clambered up the naked frame of the bird. Twin spots of flame spouted beneath each drumstick as the giant obscene image lifted slowly into the air. Shark brought his quaser to his shoulder, and almost reluctantly sighted the weapon squarely on the enemy's tailpipes; but the famished instrument of destruction sputtered its disgust, went *pfffft*, and fell apart. "They just don't make them like they used to," he noted truthfully, and tossed the remains into the gutter. The resulting explosion cleared away the already rotting bodies of the civilian casualties, saving the new government from an embarrassing change of atmosphere.

Just then, Pox wandered back to the scene, covered with assorted electrodes, resistors, and capacitors. The weird Vulgarian caressed the Captain's shoulders as he remarked: "I wonder if you have noticed, sir, how much these people resemble the Montenegrins of 19th century Earth. Having studied the history of your planetoid in great detail, I have come to the conclusion that such astonishing parallels of cultural development are not as nearly uncommon as the rationalists would have us believe. And even if it isn't true, it's an utterly fascinating concept. Man cannot avoid his destiny pedigogically." But Shark was already partially dematerialized in his hasty retreat to the ship, as the *Dingdong Belle* prepared to leave the donut world forever. "And good riddance, too," Shark yelled in fond farewell, as they passed through the hole for one last time. Colonel Wolfe was the last one up, having taken fifteen minutes out of his busy schedule to plaster the planet with turkey huts.

On the Bridge, Kulli and Oyoohoo were fighting over a quarter when Captain Shark strolled boyishly over their struggling bodies. "All right, knock it off, you two. What's the problem there, Ensign?" Kulli wiped the tears from his slanted eyes: "S-s-s-s-ir, she won't give me back my desk." "Belay it Kulli, and retire to our rec room." "Yessir." For the Captain believed that each member of his crew should have an opportunity to advance as high as his or her abilities would allow. Then again, women officers cost less, remained more docile, and were easier to manage, being less reasonable and more emotional. Since no women in the fleet were allowed to marry, most remained troubled and insecure throughout the initial stages of their careers, until bitterness hardened their hearts and minds around the age of thirty, as they realized their chances were gone forever. Their moodiness, changeability, and general lack of competence made them easy to manipulate; one only had to make cracks about their marital status and general unattractiveness to bring tears to their eyes and sobs to their noses, as they reflected in spite of themselves on the years of missed opportunities. Also, they provided a certain amount of recreation for the senior staff.

"Torque factor 69, Ensign," ordered Shark, "lay in a course for the planet Titteros." "*Ay ay ay ay, canto y no llores,*" sang Gonzales. The Captain buried his graying head in his hands: "Jeez, the help we get these days. Next thing you know they'll be wanting bullfights on the hangar deck." "Senor Capitan, I have a bleep on our long-range sensors." "Put it on the screen, Ensigno." "Si, senor." A small dot appeared on the screen in the midst of bustling stars that hurtled past at speeds no mortal man could comprehend. "Magnify." "Magnifying, sir." And the dot got bigger. "Maximum full-range amplification." "Maximum, sir." And the dot increased in size to a pinprick. Pox looked down from his science console: "Sir, unnamed censors have blacked out our reception to an astonishing degree; however, the information we have would seem to indicate a hodge-podge vessel of unknown make, origin, creed, or sex, something over two kilometres in length, and something under three in width, and something between in height. The ship is unusually massive for its size, and seems to be filled with some sort of metallic substance, except for open spaces in the Bridge and Engineering. Everything else is packed solid." Shark pondered for a moment: "We'd better take a look. Oyoohoo, open a hailing frequency to the alien vessel."

The blackess bent over her controls: All hail, alien craft; hail the summer, hail the fall, hail the great, and hail the small. Please respond on channel 19." "Damn women, they never do anything right," muttered Shark. "You-all called?" asked Lupus Wolfe, who was just appearing at the top of the escalator. "My oh my, we did have a good time on that-there planetoid. Them's right friendly folk, yessir. Now jes when's we movin' on to get mah li'l darlin' fixed?'' The ugly duckling was trailing right behind, as usual: ''Oh Daddy, I do wish you wouldn't put it quite that way. People might get the wrong impression, you know? And a girl's got her reputation to protect.'' ''And very little else,'' noted Pox from his corner. ''Oh Captain Shark,'' Miss Vajinah continued, ''I do wish you'd show me how to manipulate these controls. What, for example, does this one do?'' Her stubby little finger jabbed a button, and the craft lurched over on its side, unaccountably spilling hundreds of two-bit actors all over the decks, and completely ruining Marcel's filet mignon down in the galley. ''You might say that controls attitude,'' Shark choked, ''And my attitude is definitely becoming hostile. Colonel and Miss Wolfe, we will complete this mission in good time, since we seem to have little choice in the matter. But in the interim, we have duties to perform, and uncontrollable aliens to keep in line, and the Kringle menace to repulse, and *GODDAM IT, I CAN'T DO IT WITH YOU PEOPLE HANGING OVER MY ASS ALL THE TIME.*'' It was Jackson who alleviated the crisis: ''Com'on suh,'' he cowed, ''And you too, Miss Vee. Let's all go and play owner and slave.'' And sho'nuff, dat did da trick.

Meanwhile, Oyoohoo was fooling around again, and rapidly getting glassy-eyed, when suddenly the screen sprang into life with the picture of a little old man with a white beard and skullcap. ''Thees ees the spaceship *Moshe Dayan*, Mordecai Levin conducting. What do you want from this my humble self, I who have nothing but would give everything? Possibly, you wish to trade for my insignificant artifacts, gathered from the five corners of the galaxy, which too are of excellent construction and sometimes even worth the exorbitant prices I put upon them? You see this,'' reaching back out of view, ''I tell you, this is a first edition of one of the great books of mankind, a fantasy story of the Gods and man, an epochal play of the joys and sorrows of that tragedy called life. See, here is the title page, *The Ten Commandments*, signed with that scratchy mark right there by the author, who was very aged at the time. I make you a good price, OK? And this," reaching overhead, "ah now, this is a fine piece, very fine indeed: a shell casing actually used by the Israeli army when they stormed Karachi in 1986, just before they took over the subcontinent. A real piece of history, gentlecreatures, and cheap, oh so cheap you could not find it between here and Macrame VI. For only 15,000 USS credits, I will give you this jewel, plus, plus, an autographed picture of that famous Jewish author, H. P. Lovecraft, celebrating his 50th birthday in Jerusalem. Here it is," and he quickly flashed something in front of the camera. "Don't you ever say I didn't show you nothing. For the ladies I have something still, and very lovely you all are, I must say." He swivelled around to his left: "Gottlieb, where did it go? Ah yes, *verry* dainty, and inexpensive, ah, such a deal I would only offer to fine people like you. A genuine lamp made of Tellarine skin, fashioned by Kringle artisans in their workshops on Teufelsdrek IV. You see, it turns on like this, so, and off like this. Nice goods, huh? More, I have much more, all you gotta do is come and see...," and he continued to ramble on in an incoherent monolog that Shark found utterly fascinating.

Pox, however, was already checking the name through the ship's computer banks when a small, 3 × 5 index card popped out into his hands. Then another. And another. More and more and more, until he was shovelling mounds of them to either side. "Help," he croaked, and Shark quickly rushed over, kicked in the side of the computer, and rang up the garbage detail. Meanwhile, the alien officer was fishing around in his stacks of paper

for the right information. "Sir, this is utterly fascinating."
"I'm sure it is, Pox. Why don't you share it with the rest of us?"
"Well, Captain, only 1.32% of the human population is allergic
to chicken ova protein." "That's all very interesting, but what
about Mordecai Levin?" "Mordecai Benyamin Levin was born on
Old Earth, on July 8, 1960, somewhere in the jungles of Brooklyn,
New York, the son of a tax collector and a Jewish Princess. At
the age of nineteen, he was apprenticed to a wood carver in
Oberammergau, Bavaria, where he stayed for several years.
  After his initial period of training, he was commissioned to carve
the giant wooden cross used in the decennial passion play. Then
something happened: apparently the crosspiece fell off when they
tried to nail down the pseudo-Christ, and Levin was cursed by
the actor to wander forever until saved by the love of a true Christian girl. He hid in a garbage dump until returning to New York,
where he started a bookstore specializing in mystery and suspense
fiction (Mordecai's Morgue). When Gotham collapsed in the
Great Panic of 1984, he managed to sell his books on the black
market for toilet paper, and invested the loot in Israeli war bonds.
After the Jews took over Saudi Arabia, Africa, and India in the
Great Pogrom of 1986, Levin retired to Jerusalem, and was still
living there when He Fuk-yu established his New China Empire
in 1996. I see no further records of the name until 2036, when he
is reported selling stale cigarettes to the amphibious inhabitants
of Ylloh IV. Shall I continue, Captain?" "Enough, Pox, enough.
Christ, this schlemiel's been selling the goods for at least 900
years. What a horde he must have in that cruiser of his!" Pox
connoted: "The more remote the effect from the cause, Captain,
the more extensive its possibilities. One should never seek trouble
unless it is far off." "Sounds good, Pox. Oyoohoo, inform Rabbi
Levin that we're beaming aboard for an inspection. Pox, you'll

have the conn in my absence; I'll be taking Hoyle, Shoddy, and Randy; have them report to the transceiver room."

Commander Ward was waiting for them when Shark arrived. "I'm ha'in' a wee bit o' difficulty, sar, with the thermionic mono-molecular hypochondrium, but I think I can get her to wark with a chunk o' Ilang-Ilang vesuvianite." He grinned that engineer's smile of his, and skillfully tossed the rock into the jumble of wires, transistors, and vacuum tubes that marked the heart of the gadget; the resulting sparks and flames took three special effects tech-nicians nine days to clean up. As the smoke drifted away, Shod-dy's blackened face glowed at them out of the dark, like a street lamp in the London fog: "I think I've found the trouble, Cap'n; it's the dextrorse antixerophthalmic radiator. It should wark fine now." The Serbocroatian Scotch-Irish-English Welshman reached down, twiddled his thumbs, crossed his T wires, and finally flicked his bitch before vanishing in the haze. Somehow he got to the launching pads before lift-off. After a moment's pause for a paid political announcement, the four spacemen flickered into life on the Bridge of the *Moshe Dayan*. For a second, Shark had the odd sense of being slightly out of place. Then he realized that every-thing was perfectly normal--for a Hindu. Each of the crew had exchanged bodies with someone else.

"Welcome, Captain Shark, welcome to this my humble temple. My, you are a strange one, aren't you? Well well well, we never let such things interfere with business. Now, before we begin, I wish to make my establishment perfectly clear. We are all honest men, I know; however, the rules of the house state quite clearly"--he handed each of the spacemen a printed sheet--"that we only accept cash on the line: no credit cards, no checks, no funny money, OK? Now what can I do for you, my friends?" The little schwartzbaum cracked his cheeks in a warped caricature of a smile.

Annie Randy had finally recovered from her faint reply: "You don't seem to understand, Mr. Levin: h-he's got my body!" "You want that I should weep, maybe? Jehovah's witnesses, what these gentiles expect from an old man. What way is it supposed to be, huh? Oh yes, yes, I see it now, you over there go here, and that one over here goes somewhere else. Tellya what I'm gonna do. Such a deal I don't just offer to everybody, you betch your life, But first, I'm gonna need 50,000 credits apiece--gold coin, please-- to do the job. Yes yes, I know that's a lotta money, but transplants don't come cheap these days: there's the spare parts, oy, they cost a fortune! And good labor, it is so hard to find. Inflation, and the taxes, oh the taxes, you just would not believe it. Besides, it's a risky business: I could get sued for malpractice maybe. And my insurance man, he's got a wife and kids to support. And my 46 ex-wives, all their lawyers want their alimony checks. Please understand, I don't like making all this money, but a business is a business: it's not a charity, see? You just don't know what it is to be a simple trader these days." Miss Shark exchanged glances with all her companions, then calmly opened her communicator: "Pox, we're gonna need some help over here." "Thank you, yeo-person," was the reply, "Now if you will get me the Captain...." "Pox, please. This is most...difficult. Hmmmmm. I am the Captain of the *Dingdong Belle*, I have a mer...." "Enough, sir, I just wanted to make sure." The gold was swiftly moved between the two vessels.

As soon as the ancient rabbi had finished counting out his thalers, he turned to his clients, and motioned them into the transceiver port. "You und you," he said, pointing to Shark and Randy. "Now, lemme see, it's been awhile." He started leafing through his manual, *How to Use Your Transceiver More Ef-*

ficiently, by Solomon G. Rossman. "Ah yes, here it is. Place finger B on knob J, and turn J three-quarters of a revolution to letter Y. Just so. Then pull out knob Q until it pops loose, and eat it. Match wire DF with end of string GX. Scramble. Now say the words, 'Paracelsus, Tegucigalpa, Maracaibo,' and throw the whole works into a tub. Ha!" Shark and the yeoperson faded away in a mutual orgasm of golden bangles and beads, then slowly came back to their completely nude bodies. "Again, Junius, again," murmured Annie, her pale lips glossy with the dew of a thousand lovestorms. "My gypsy moth," Shark replied hushedly, and smothered her in his aching arms. "Later, children, later," said the old Jew, "I have a contract to keep. Out, out, stand over there, please; and you other two, you get in," motioning to Shoddy and Hoyle. Soon the four of them were romping around the *Moshe Dayan* like kids in a nudist park. The white-bearded Faust threw up his dinner in disgust: "Listen, you want that I should entertain you? This is a business establishment: you don't wanna buy nothin', you get the hell out. I got no time for freeloaders. Come on, move along, into the transceiver, all of yous. Here, little lady, here's a present for you, a token of my small esteem, a nice little furry thing. You like it, huh? Yeah, well, I call it a wibble. Batsdrek, Captain, you want something too? Oy vey, they're all mercenaries here. How's a poor trader to live? All right, all right, here's a bumper sticker from the edge of the galaxy. They gotta barbed wire fence and a hot dog stand there; they don't let anyone out. Why? How should I know why? It was nice meeting you too. Goodbye please." After the crewmen had gone, the crafty old thing smiled: "That was a pretty good haul, eh, Gottlieb? Look what we got here: the uniforms alone should get at least a hundred apiece to the Kringle crowd, and the quasers I can sell anywhere. Not so hot in the quality line, maybe, but goods is goods." He was chuckling merrily to himself for weeks afterward.

With the four crewpersons back on the Bridge, things more or less got back to normal, until Pox pointed out the precession of the equinoxes, which must have meant something. Yeoperson Randy had stuffed the wibble down the front of her plunging neckline, to keep it warm. "May I pet it?" asked Fuckoff, and without waiting for a reply, began to stroke the furry thing where it lay tucked between her warm, generous breasts. Somehow the clumsy peasant managed to get more of Annie than he did of the animal, but you can't keep a good Russian down. "There are two of them," he murmured lasciviously, grasping and groaning with the effort; and sho'nuff, there were now a pair of the fluffy balls covering Randy's white, steaming flesh. As they all stared with delight at the girl's once-hidden wonders, two more of the hairy monsters sprang into view, and then a third, fourth, and fifth. Shark slammed his fist down on his knee: "Get me Lupus Wolfe right away," he ordered. Several hours, and thousands of wibbles later, Wolfe finally managed to crawl his way up the jammed escalator. "You-all said it was urgent," he noted. Shark was standing on his chair, gazing down at the surging sea of wibbles: "Just take a took at these, Wolfe, and tell me what you think." "Well, Cap'n, I gotta say, that's the finest pair of knockers I've seen this side of the Mississipp." "You may have something there, Wolfe; but I'm beginning to wonder whether either of us will live long enough to enjoy them." Miss Vajinah was rolling around on the floor, covered with the copulating parasites, huffing and puffing her delight: "Oh Daddy, I ain't never felt this way 'bout no one." "Maybe you oughta marry one, dear," her father replied; "That way, neither of us would ever be lonely again." "Oh Daddy, do you really think so? Ohhh,

Daaady!'' Meanwhile, the leading wibbles were building wibble houses on Pox's science console, and others were playing tag with the two fruity helmspersons, and things were rapidly going from worse to knockwurst. Captain Shark realized that firm action had to be taken, so he pulled out his quaser, and started frying the little buggers where they lay. "Not bad," noted Pox, as he took a bite out of a typical burnt-out case. But Randy was shocked: "Junius, how could you?" she cried. "I'll never let you show me your dirty pictures ever again. They're just so soft and cuddly and cushy, like a new roll of toilet paper. You can't just kill them." With the rest of the crew threatening mutiny, Shark abandoned the Bridge, and ordered his chief officers to assemble in the back-up control room. "Gentlepersons," he prompted, "I need some ideas." "Aye, Cap'n, let's get drunk," Shoddy plinked, pulling a bottle of Scotch out of his britches. The Rev. Mr. Hoyle had a better idea: "Let's get the wibbles drunk, bless their souls." But his suggestion was hooted down as a waste of good liquor. It was Pox who had the final solution: "Captain, I have often noted that a blind man should feel his head with a cane before proceeding. It follows by inverse progression that substituting two vats of mesognathous parturifacient would sap the creatures' energy to the point where they could be force fed with bingle-berries. And, as the Captain surely knows, there is no cure for bingleberry poisoning." Yeoperson Randy was placated with the promise of a wibble fur coat.

Soon, the lovely smell of rotting wibbles had permeated the en-tire craft, and on each deck men and women and things coped with the situation in their own initimable ways. One poor creature from Gyro IX carried his head around in a bucket of water for days and days, trying to find the bathroom. The few wibbles who had managed to wibble their way out of the trap were scooped up in forklifts, hog-tied into bales of hay, and beamed aboard a passing freighter. It was a neat ending to a perfect day. "I must say, son," Wolfe cigarred, "You-all handled the situation as good as any Suthrun politician coulda done." "Thanks, Wolfe, you aren't so bad yourself," Shark replied, and they soon fell into each others' arms, exploring the possibilities of a long and fruitful relationship.

Their tete-a-tete was interrupted by Kulli's report: "Bogey's at twelve o'clock!" "What's he doin' here?" asked Wolfe. "You-all put it on that-there screen, boy." Grazing amidst the clovered fields of stars and stripes was a small moving dot, which quickly resolved itself into the giant figure of a horse. "My god," said the Captain, "What the hell is that!" Open a hailing frequency, Oyoohoo." "Aye aye, sir." "Any response, communications-person?" "Neigh, Captain, nary a word." "Wolfe, I think you'd better handle this one. I'll be in my sauna bath." The fat Missourian settled his bulk into the control chair: "All right now, boy, I wantchya to fasten a tractor beam onto her nose, and bring her in real slow like." "She's fighting it rather hard, sir, bucking and pulling." "Jes keep her steady, son; ya gotta break her spirit if you're gonna get her into that hangar. Don't let her get away with anything, now. Pull her in, pull her in, that's the way, almost there. *Yippee! We done it!*" Wolfe hurried down to the hangar bay, and rushed into the now-pressurized football field. Standing tall above the officers, like some ancient Greek god, was the giant statue of a horse on wheels, a silver-studded saddle draped over its back. "Hey you, Lox or whatever your name is, whatchya-all think of this-here animule?" "Frankly, sir, I would not wish to meet the owner of this vehicle in an alley after dark. He is, I think you would say, a momentous event. I have, however, noticed one peculiarity," and he pointed to the base of the right front leg, where the initials *USC* were quite plainly scratched into the unknown metal alloy. "What's it all mean, Sox?" "Pox, sir, if you please. Obviously, this is a kabbalistic device meant to confuse and intimidate us. We can assume that the letters are either an abbreviation, or that they stand for something else. A negative syllogism should not rule out the possibility of alphabetical polytheism. I would suggest one likely solution, the United Streetsweepers of Calexico, on the grounds that someone has to clean up the residue left by mobile transportation, and undoubtedly this image was erected in gratitude by the citizens of Cucamonga." Lupus Wolfe considered it a moment, and said: "That's a crocka horse-shit." "I, uh, well, I-I-I t-t-try to speak wisely and pithily and meaningfully, as I was taught to do in high school. I was never well-liked, sir, even then, and it is difficult to know precisely what to say. I'm alien and human, A/C and D/C, logical and il-. Everyone else knows who he or she or it is, but not Pox. It's just that... no one understands. And...no one cares. I am all alone in the universe, with no one to love but myself." Unconsciously, he manipulated the computer controls to produce a weird sort of electronic accompaniment, as he warbled:

> *"Poor little Mr. Pox,*
> *Weird little Mr. Pox,*
> *With his emotions repressed.*
> *Odd little Mr. Pox,*
> *Queer little Mr. Pox,*
> *Clothed in a vulcanized dress."*

"I wrote it myself, sir," he sobbed, falling into Wolfe's horrified arms. "Now, now, Cox," paternosterized Wolfe, patting him between the ears. "Ain't there someone else here who could do this?" he whispered to Shoddy, but the engineer just shrank away. No one particularly liked Pox; no one particularly cared. "Well now," the old farmer said, drying away the tears, "It's been a long day for everybody, so let's close up shop. We'll corral this-here creature tomorrow. Savvy?" And they all went beddie-bye.

When Shark's alarm clock exploded at 0600 hours, he shut the damn thing off, rolled over, and went back to sleep. It was only three or four hours later that he realized no one had come to draw his hot morning bath. "Gods, the draftees we get these days," he muttered half-consciously; "I suppose I ought to get up." But a shadowy figure insinuated itself between him and the 100-watt bulb glaring nakedly down from the ceiling, and a warm, soft arm crept around his neck: "Silly Captain Shark," the beautiful alien chirped, "Did you really think you could resist the advances of the Meansis?" Shark shook his head vigorously, and then succumbed.

After completely destroying the officer's moral fibres, Yram Ecila took Shark to the Bridge, where he saw first hand the damage wrought by the aliens' Graineyator. His finely-honed crew of 333 men, women and things had been reduced to moldy chunks of Wheerios, Tost Posties, Raisin Rind, Kringle-berries, and doggie-doo. The aliens had evidently secreted themselves in the great body of the horse, and had emerged sometime during the night, quickly overpowering the key personnel of the ship. They now had complete control of the *Dingdong Belle*, or so they claimed, and had begun altering the cafeteria converters to their own nefarious ends. "What I don't understand," Shark rumbled, "is why?"

"Why indeed," replied the stargirl. "You see, human, we are not really aliens at all, but onetime people like yourself, who have been subverted by political doctrines into neolithic propagandizers. We have appropriated your bourgeois ship to protest your cruel and inhuman treatment of minority groups." "Minority groups? What minority groups? Christ, this whole place is run by minority groups." Yram Ecila placed her dainty little fingers over Shark's thing. "We find you underrepresented, dear Captain Shark, in these respects: no American Indians...." "But there aren't any more American Indians," Shark interrupted. "*No* American Indians (of which I am one), no Serbo-Croatians except for one half-breed, no Know Nothings, no members of the Saudi Arabia Women's League, no one from the Save the Pigeon Federation of Ulan Bator, no one from the Valley of Ten Thousand Smokes, no android representing the robot population of Peenemunde, nobody from the Ex-Dictators Coalition, and utterly no being, Captain, from the Restore George III Movement of Valley Forge." "An impressive list, Miss Ecila." "Yram, please. We have been protesting these inequities for at least 900 years, Captain Shark, and we will continue to travel the galactic airspaces for 900 more, if necessary. We will never submit. And now, Captain, we have taken over your ship for a very special reason: we are diverting it to the Peoples' Space Park near Titteros III, where we will dismantle all of your weapons and engines, and convert the *Dingdong Belle* into a free organic pizza dispensary."

Shark was amazed at their audacity, and nearly missed his command chair as he slumped down in desperation. "You see, Captain, you're the only one on board who's really necessary for the operation of this vessel: we need you to help navigate. We tried getting the rest to do it, but either they didn't know how, or they refused to help without higher orders. And you will help, Shark, or...." She reached behind the Captain's seat, and drew out a bowl full of Crewmen Crispies, and calmly started pouring milk and sugar over the contents. "Care for a bite, Captain?" Yram inquired, as she started scooping globs of Gonzales into her pouch. "Hear that snap, crackle, and pop?" "All right, all right,

I'll do what you want. But you'll have to restore my crew first, before I do anything. Otherwise you can take that device of yours, and convert me as well, because I won't budge a millimeter longer." The Indian princess agreed, and soon the crew (all except for Gonzales) were back doing their things.

Shark was invited to a powwow with the Indian leaders, and brought along Pox and Wolfe. "How," said the chief. "How," replied the spacemen. "I am Siddhartha Means," intoned the old man gravely, "Chief of the AIPP." "Pardon me, sir," Pox queried, "just what is the AIPP?" "Greenface, you are one of much ignorance and much wisdom. My daughter, answer my friend." "American Indian Pooh-Pooh." "How," intoned the old man, "I am Siddhartha Means, Chief of the AIPP. The members of my council are sitting with me at this table." "How, I am Hare Krishna Means, Chief of the Sub-Council of Five." "How, I am Waysand Means, Chief of the Gitchie Goomies." "How, I am Means-to-an-End, Sub-Chief of the Kulturikampfi." "How, I am Georgia Means, Chieftess of Los Angeles." "How, I am Raksharajah Means, Meanest of the Means." "How, I am Yram Ecila Means, daughter of the Great Chief, and sexpot of the Kalihari." "How," they all chanted, "We are of all Means, by all Means, for all Means, and shall not perish from this earth." "But you're out in space," Shark noted.

"Great White Leader," groaned Siddhartha Means, "what is your name?" "Junius Torquemada Shark, serial number TB-007-1984-Bu-8, Captain, *USS Dingdong Belle*." "Then, sir, we have met face-to-face on the battlefields of perdition and honor, and the enemy is ours. Don't give up the ship; we regret that we have but one lie to lend to our countrymen. Tarry me not in the lone priory. There is no god but Kampala, and Edie Amino is his profit. In other words, since we can't bury our hatchets in your

thick skulls, why not forget them together in clouds of smokum?''
"What the hell is he talking about?" Shark asked Wolfe. "Beats
me," replied the plantation owner. "Sounds to me like he's been
down on the funny farm once too often, if you-all knows what I
mean." "That's the way it sounds to me, too. Hey look, you guys,
I appreciate everything you're saying, and we just happen to be
heading in the direction of Titteros anyway. You're welcome to
ride along. But I can't let you have this ship, because if I did,
the dogs would start barking in the night, and you know what that
means." Pox picked up the cue: "Well, sir, you will recall that
the dog is man's best friend. It follows, therefore, that a puppy
cannot see the nut's contents until his shell is cracked." Wolfe
followed: "Your possessive is indeterminate, Pox, and therefore
inoperative. You have failed primary logic, and must return to
Deduction 412. Thou shalt not compute thy neighbor's wife. Keep
holy the Toad's day. Analyzed?" "Coded, sir. I mesh." "And
may all your bits be little ones," Shark yelled, as he leaped for
the Graineyators fastened on the Chief's belt. "What shall we do
with them, sir?" Pox inquired, after the last of the Indians had
fallen to the alien handgrip. "Put 'em in the brig, mister. We'll
let them loose again on Titteros III."

Two days later, Fuckoff reported multiple contacts on the scanners. "Captain," he quiensabed, "my readings indicate several
thousand spacecraft clustered more or less around one medium-
sized asteroid. I've also picked up many smaller pieces of rock,
and what appears to be fragments of litter scattered haphazardly
through this particular belt. How do you wish to proceed?"
"I don't like it. Slow to torque factor one, Fuckoff." "Aye, Captain." The Titteros system was located in the Culdesac Nebula,
and it had a bad reputation, even among spacemen. The Peoples'
Space Park had been set up centuries before by a group of hippie

exiles from the Terran worlds, and had gradually accumulated a population of deadbeats, conmen, and hustlers, who moved from junked ship to junked ship in an ever-ending search for pleasure and an easy buck. Titteros owed allegiance to none of the great empires, and had managed to keep its independence because it was a useful buffer between the Kringles and the United Systems, being one of the few places in the galaxy where earthmen and Kringles could mingle freely if they so desired. It was also the center of several intergalactic smuggling rings. By virtue of the Kringle-Terran Treaty of 2864, Titteros was included in the buffer zone between the two states, and battle cruisers were forbidden to approach any closer than a million kilometres.

"Dead stop, Fuckoff. Oyoohoo, ask Colonel Wolfe and his daughter to come to the Bridge, please. Pox, do you know where the alien toad is?" "Sir, I believe he was taken ill shortly after coming on board, and Dr. Sobhuza finally put him under sedation for the duration of the trip, except for the one time when he had to make an appearance on Circus III." "Very well, ask the good doctor to restore him to consciousness, and bring him to the Bridge." "Yes, Captain,"

"Long range scanners on, Kulli." "Scanners on, Sir," and on the viewscreen there appeared the great glowing globe of the orange planetoid, Titteros III. "What's that mark in the Southern hemisphere, Pox?" "Sir, information in our computer banks indicates that most of the asteroid has been hollowed out for living quarters; there appears to be a large airlock through which small shuttlecraft can directly enter the planet's skin; the dark area around the lock is the radar/tractor beam system which guides the craft in. No space vehicle is allowed to approach Titteros itself under internal power." "Touchy, aren't they?"

At that moment, the Colonel and Miss Vajinah arrived, breathless, the both of them, and the horny toad, still bemoaning its fate: "Oh gentlebeingth, I get *thooo* thpathethick."

Shark swivelled slowly around in his command chair: "All right, people, we're here, and I must say, I don't like it a bit. First of all, we shouldn't be anywhere near this sector. If the Kringles find us here,they have every right to try to shoot us out of the sky. And secondly, I don't like the thought of going in there"--he pointed to the screen--"To do whatever it is we have to do. And right about now, I want to know just what that is."

"Well, suh," Wolfe responded, "it's my byutiful daughter, Miss Vajinah, who needs a little, uh, molecular reconstruction, if you-all knows what I mean. And this-here thing promised to do it for me." "Will you explain, please?" asked the Captain. "Yeth. I was forthed to bring you here by thith cruel, cruel human-perthon, who hath my pathport, and won't let me go.

"Many eonth ago, I happened to frequent thith planet on a bithneth trip, and oh my, had a minor dithagreement with thome colleagueth of mine. They were heartlethth men, and the ultimate punithment on Titteroth ith not death, ath on other worldth, but reconthtituthion. For you thee, gentlebeingth, when they emptied that world, they made a great dithcovery, an alien artifact left by thome race forgotten by the ageth. Thith devithe ith a molecular thynthethizer, which enabled itth dithcovererth to itholate the Titteroth thythem, and make it independently wealthy; the directorth of the thythtem are rich men. The motht important thing for them wath thecrethy, for if the Kringleth or humanth had found out about it, they would have fought to the death for itth powerful poththibilitieth. Tho the thyndicate advertithed in thtrange wayth, and one by one, old and dying thtatethmen and bithnethmen would find their wayth to Titteroth, and pay their feeth, and go away whole again, their memorieth wiped clean.

I found out about the devithe, and tried to blackmail the thyn-dicate; but they kidnapped me, and brought me to the thentral control room, where they changed me into the form you thee here, and told me that if I ever told anyone, I would never have the chanthe to change back. Tho I have wandered galactic thpace for hundredth of yearth, afraid to mention a word, and doing what-ever they told me, until you forthed me to divulge my thecret. And now, you mutht promithe me, that if I take you to the control room, and show you how to uthe the devithe, you will change me back to my original form, and let me go free afterwardth, far away from here." "You have my word," promised Shark.

"Pox." "Sir?" "How close can we get before they pick us up?" "I doubt their equipment is as sophisticated as ours, Captain, but I wouldn't want to go much closer, I think. They can probably detect us now, as a foreign object a certain distance away, but I doubt they can tell exactly who or what we are." "That's all I wanted to know. Oyoohoo, open a hailing frequency to Titteros III, audio only, please." A quavering voice responded: "Alien vessel, this is Titteros Command Control. Identify your-selves." Shark jabbed the communications button forcefully: "This is the United Systems Freighter *Dingdong Belle*, requesting permission to land a trading craft on the Titteros main dock." "Permission granted, *Belle*. Proceed on course 268.3, mark 7." Shark turned to the crew: "I want the shuttlecraft repainted and renamed the *Virginia Clark*. We're going as traders, so have the ship's tailor supply the appropriate clothing. Pox, I'll want you and Hoyle with me. Shoddy'll have the conn. Let's move it, lads."

Within an hour, the shuttlecraft was skirting the first of the derelict space vehicles surrounding the planetoid. "Captain, look there," Pox motioned. Far to the right as they swept past a line of occupied craft was the golden arch of a Kringle klutch. "Shit," Shark shivered, "That means there's a cruiser around somewhere. They must have gotten wind of the synthesizer. We're likely to encounter them on the planet, too. Be sure your quasers are loaded and charged."

Soon they were approaching the great circular opening leading to the landing locks of Titteros. The *Virginia Clark* came to a rest with a bump. "Artifical gravity on, Captain." "OK, Pox; keep your weapons hidden until necessary." and he opened the hatch with a switch. "Gentlebeingth," Nethtor whithpered, "we have to take the shuttletubeth," and he led them over to an opening. "Secret synthesizer, Central Control Station," Shark called out, and off they went with a whoosh. With another whoosh, they were unceremoniously dumped out onto the pavement. They were in a small square; across from them was a guarded entranceway marked "Central Control"; to the left was a park, and to the right another Klutch. "My god," shouted Hoyle, "the Kurnel's got wibs!" and sho'nuff, spread all over the front bench were mounds of wibbleburgers, splashed gloriously with parsley, mustard, and the Kurnel's secret sauce. Just then Kurnel himself, dressed up in a cook's frock, spotted them through the open window of his shop, and with an oath, snatched up his Kringlekork, and let blaze. *Zap!* went the gun, and *crack!* went the shuttlecar, as it melted away into the pavement. The guards across the way pulled their own weapons, and shot down the golden horseshoe over the hut. With the two sides shooting at each other, Shark motioned his party towards the unprotected entrance to the synthesizer, and headed for shelter.

Once inside, Nethtor led them down a series of corridors until they came to one marked: *Absolutely no entrance save by authorized personnel, and then only on Fridays.* They melted open the door, and warped in. Lying on a card table in the center of the room was a small metal box. Shark walked over, opened it, and looked at the ring lying inside. "Why, it's just a cheap stone," he said. "It looks like artifical glass." And he held it up to a green light on the nearest wall.

WHAT DO YOU WISH?" it thundered. Miss Vajinah Wolfe waltzed over: "All I want for Christmas is my two front teats," she sang in a pseudo-falsetto. The ring began to glow with an emerald hue, and twin beams reached out and touched the girl there and there, and then her blouse began to bulge until it reached its outer limits, and split completely asunder. "My god," Shark cried, but god had nothing to do with the 42-inch globes that stood ponderously out from the girl's slender frame.

"WHAT DO YOU WISH?" asked the voice. "Oh my good-neththth," lithped the toad, "I wanna be meee, just wanna be meeeee...." Again the ring glowed green, and again the beam reached out to touch the great amphibian. And suddenly the toad was gone, and in its place was the fat, sweaty frame of Mammy Jumbo: "Well I declaire, yo' sho'nuff was fooled by ol' Mammy, now wasn't you? And you there, Lupus Wolfe, you got what you wishes?"

"Now jes a friggin' minute, you old charlatan, I had one more wish that you-all ain't done nothin' about, and that's gettin' my poor darlin' a hubby." "Ho ho ho, Lupus, I didn't say nothin' 'bout no hubby for Miz Vajinah. All I said was dat she would marry da one of her choice. Ain't dat right sweetheart? Now Miz Vajinah..."--"WHAT DO YOU WISH? commanded the ring-- "is a Lesbo, as I well knows, an' she don't want no man, now do you honey?" "No ma'am. I never really like men very much. They're all so...sweaty and filthy, if you know what I mean. They all want to make love with their things. And I never wanted to go out with them, at least with any of the straight ones, because I might have to actually feel something then, and I'd rather hide somewheres in a corner, and bemoan my fate. You see, Daddy, I never really loved any man but you. No man could possibly be as good as that, or as rich. So I stayed home, and played with my dogs, except when I met someone I knew wouldn't touch me, like the fag artist across the road. I'd let him take me out, because he was safe. And the rest of the time I either diddled away my frustrations, or got off with the girls. I like my Mammy," and she cuddled up close to those ponderous globes of hers.

At that moment, the Kringle Kommander Kurnel pushed through the door: "Finally, Shark, I will get my revenge. All of you line up against the wall." "Uh, Kurnel, I wouldn't like to see those dirty locks of yours messed up. So why don't you just drop that raygun and we'll each go our merry ways." Kurnel laughed his vicious laugh: "The day a Kringle takes orders from a barbarian like you is the day we'll all go to the dogs." Shark smiled: "I wish you would, my friend." The ring in his hand began pulsing once more, and suddenly zapped the alien with its green ray; where the Kringle had stood was the friendly, panting face of a bluetick hound, who quietly loped over and licked Shark's hand. The Captain pulled out his transceiver: "Shoddy, get us out of here," he yelled, and a moment later, just as the local gendarmes appeared, they all disappeared in a flurry of tinsel.

Back on the *Dingdong Belle*, Shark was safe once more in his command chair, nuzzling the breasts of Yeoperson Randy. "So much for war," he whispered softly into her lambent ears, "and now for the love part...." "What I fail to understand, sir," said Pox in his unobtrusively obnoxious way, "is how we ever got out of this mess. It's obvious that the intelligent defense of one's rationales is the best guarantee of peace. Still, unknown danger is like the summer's junebug: it strikes where least expected,'' and truer words could not have been spoken, as the enterprising starmen would soon find out, in *The Grapefruit of the Galaxy*; or, *The Stars Are Ripe Forever*. But Shark was too busy for words, and the rest was brillig in the astrolobes.

The Milford Series:
Popular Writers of Today

1. *Robert A. Heinlein: Stranger in His Own Land* [second edition, revised], by George Edgar Slusser.
2. *Alistair MacLean: The Key Is Fear*, by Robert A. Lee.
3. *The Farthest Shores of Ursula K. Le Guin*, by George Edgar Slusser.
4. *The Bradbury Chronicles*, by George Edgar Slusser.
5. *John D. MacDonald and the Colorful World of Travis McGee*, by Frank D. Campbell, Jr.
6. *Harlan Ellison: Unrepentant Harlequin*, by George Edgar Slusser.
7. *Kurt Vonnegut: The Gospel from Outer Space (or, Yes We Have No Nirvanas)*, by Clark Mayo [Oct. 1977].
8. *The Space Odysseys of Arthur C. Clarke*, by George Edgar Slusser [Oct. 1977].
9. *Aldiss Unbound: The Science Fiction of Brian W. Aldiss*, by Richard Mathews [Oct. 1977].
10. *The Delany Intersection: Samuel R. Delany Considered As a Writer of Semi-Precious Words*, by George Edgar Slusser [Oct. 1977].
11. *The Classic Years of Robert A. Heinlein*, by George Edgar Slusser [Oct. 1977].

Other Borgo Press publications:

a. *The Beach Boys: Southern California Pastoral*, by Bruce Golden.
b. *The Attempted Assassination of John F. Kennedy*, a science fiction novel by Lucas Webb.
c. *Up Your Asteroid! A Science Fiction Farce*, by C. Everett Cooper.
d. *Hasan*, a fantasy novel by Piers Anthony [Oct. 1977; $3.95].

Available for $1.95 each [except where indicated], plus postage and handling, from The Borgo Press, P.O. Box 2845, San Bernardino, California 92406. California residents add 6% sales tax.

www.ingramcontent.com/pod-product-compliance
Lightning Source LLC
Chambersburg PA
CBHW050914120626
46552CB00004B/1575